MARCILLINUS ASOGWA

Leading from Within: Unleashing Your Inner Potential

Contents

1

The Call to Action

The dimly lit room hummed with anticipation as the clock ticked towards midnight. Papers rustled in the stale air, casting long shadows over the worn wooden floor. In the corner, a lone figure hunched over a cluttered desk, the flickering light of a candle casting eerie shadows across their face. This was Michael Stone, a man haunted by the ghosts of his past and driven by a relentless desire to unlock his inner potential.

For years, Michael had toiled away in obscurity, struggling to make ends meet in a world that seemed determined to crush his dreams. But tonight was different. Tonight, an invitation had arrived—an invitation promising a chance at prosperity, a chance to break free from the chains of mediocrity and step into a world of limitless possibilities.

As Michael traced the words on the crumpled piece of paper, a surge of excitement coursed through his veins. The seminar promised to reveal the secrets of success, to unlock the hidden potential that lay dormant within each and every one of them. It was an opportunity too tantalizing to ignore, too promising to pass up.

With a sense of determination burning in his chest, Michael rose from his seat and made his way to the door. The streets outside were quiet, shrouded in darkness and mystery. But Michael paid no heed to the shadows that lurked in the corners; his mind was consumed with thoughts of what lay ahead.

The journey to the seminar was long and arduous, the streets winding and unfamiliar. But with each step, Michael felt a renewed sense of purpose, a flicker of hope igniting within him like a flame in the darkness. He was ready to embrace whatever challenges lay ahead, ready to seize the opportunity that had been presented to him.

Finally, after what seemed like an eternity, Michael arrived at his destination—a nondescript building nestled in the heart of the city. The doors loomed before him, imposing and grand, as if daring him to step inside and face his destiny.

With a deep breath, Michael pushed open the doors and stepped into the unknown. The room beyond was bathed in warm light, the air thick with anticipation and excitement. People bustled about, their voices a low murmur in the background as they exchanged nervous glances and whispered words of encouragement.

Michael found himself drawn towards the front of the room, where a stage had been set up with a single podium standing proudly in the center. As he took his seat among the eager crowd, he couldn't help but feel a sense of awe wash over him. This was it—the beginning of a journey that would change his life forever.

Little did Michael know, the path to prosperity would be fraught with peril and uncertainty, testing him in ways he could never have imagined. But as he sat there in the glow of the stage lights, surrounded by strangers who shared his hopes and dreams, he knew that he was ready to face whatever challenges lay ahead. For Michael Stone, the journey had only just begun.

2

The Enigmatic Mentor

The morning sun cast a golden hue over the city as Michael Stone navigated the bustling streets, his mind still reeling from the events of the previous night. The seminar had been a revelation, a glimpse into a world of endless possibilities and untapped potential. But as he made his way towards the designated meeting spot, a sense of unease gnawed at his gut.

The address led Michael to a nondescript alleyway, where a lone figure stood waiting in the shadows. As Michael approached, the figure stepped forward, revealing himself to be a tall, imposing man with piercing eyes and a disarming smile. This was Marcus Blackwood, the enigmatic mentor who would guide Michael on his journey of self-discovery.

With a curt nod, Marcus beckoned for Michael to follow him into the depths of the city. They walked in silence for what felt like hours, the sounds of the bustling metropolis fading into the background as they ventured further from the beaten path. Finally, they arrived at their destination—a secluded warehouse on the outskirts of town, its windows boarded up and its doors padlocked shut.

As Marcus produced a set of keys from his pocket and unlocked the door, Michael's heart raced with anticipation. What secrets lay hidden within this desolate place? What mysteries awaited him on the other side?

The interior of the warehouse was dark and musty, the air thick with the scent of decay. Marcus led Michael through a labyrinth of corridors and staircases, their footsteps echoing off the walls like whispers in the night. Finally, they reached a small room at the heart of the building, where a single chair sat illuminated by a dim overhead light.

With a gesture, Marcus motioned for Michael to take a seat. As he did, Marcus began to speak, his voice low and hypnotic, like a siren's song luring Michael deeper into the unknown.

"You seek prosperity, Michael," Marcus intoned, his eyes boring into Michael's soul with an intensity that sent shivers down his spine. "But prosperity comes at a price—a price that few are willing to pay."

As Marcus spoke, Michael felt a strange sense of unease wash over him. Who was this man, and what did he know of the price of prosperity? And more importantly, what role did he play in Michael's journey towards success?

But before Michael could voice his concerns, Marcus reached into his pocket and produced a small vial filled with a shimmering liquid. With a flourish, he offered it to Michael, his lips curling into a knowing smile.

"This is the key to unlocking your inner potential, Michael," Marcus said, his voice dripping with honeyed promises. "But be warned—once you take this step, there is no turning back. Are you prepared to face the truth, no matter how dark it may be?"

Michael hesitated, his mind racing with doubts and fears. But deep down, he knew that this was his chance—a chance to break free from the shackles of his past and embrace a future filled with promise and possibility.

With a trembling hand, he reached out and took the vial from Marcus, his fingers closing around it like a vice. And as he did, he felt a surge of power coursing through his veins, filling him with a sense of purpose and determination unlike anything he had ever known.

But little did Michael realize, the path to prosperity was fraught with danger and deception, and Marcus Blackwood held the key to unlocking not only Michael's inner potential, but also the dark secrets that lay hidden within his own soul. As they embarked on this journey together, the lines between mentor and mentee would blur, and Michael would soon come to realize that the true cost of prosperity was far greater than he could ever have imagined.

3

The Trials Begin

As the sun dipped below the horizon, casting long shadows across the city, Michael Stone found himself standing before a towering edifice—an ancient mansion nestled in the heart of the forest, its ivy-covered walls whispering secrets of a bygone era. This was the first trial on his journey towards unlocking his inner potential, and as he gazed up at the imposing facade, a shiver of apprehension ran down his spine.

With a deep breath, Michael stepped through the wrought-iron gates and into the overgrown garden beyond. The air was thick with the scent of moss and decay, the only sound the crunch of leaves beneath his feet as he made his way towards the entrance.

Inside, the mansion was cloaked in darkness, the air heavy with the weight of centuries. Cobwebs adorned the walls like gossamer tapestries, and the faint drip of water echoed through the halls like a melancholy melody. But Michael paid no heed to the eerie atmosphere; his mind was focused on the task at hand.

As he ventured deeper into the mansion, he came upon a series of rooms, each more foreboding than the last. In one, he faced a riddle of impossible complexity, his mind racing to unravel its enigmatic clues. In another, he encountered a labyrinth of mirrors, each reflecting a different aspect of his own soul.

But it was the final room that held the greatest challenge—a chamber bathed in an ethereal light, its walls adorned with symbols of arcane power. At the center of the room stood a pedestal, upon which rested a single, shimmering orb—the key to unlocking Michael's inner potential.

With a sense of determination burning in his chest, Michael approached the pedestal and reached out for the orb. But as his fingers closed around its smooth surface, a sudden gust of wind swept through the room, extinguishing the torches and plunging him into darkness.

Panic surged through Michael's veins as he groped blindly in the darkness, his heart pounding in his chest. But just as he began to lose hope, a voice echoed through the darkness—a voice he recognized as Marcus Blackwood's.

"Do not be afraid, Michael," the voice whispered, its tone both soothing and commanding. "This is your moment of truth, a test of your strength and resolve. Embrace the darkness, and you will find the light."

With those words ringing in his ears, Michael closed his eyes and let go of his fear. And as he did, he felt a surge of power coursing through his veins, illuminating the darkness like a beacon of hope. With newfound clarity, he reached out once more for the orb, and this time, his fingers closed around it with certainty and purpose.

As the darkness receded and the torches flickered back to life, Michael found himself standing once more in the chamber, the orb pulsing with an inner light in his hand. And as he looked upon it, he knew that he had passed the first trial on his journey towards unlocking his inner potential.

But little did Michael know, the challenges that lay ahead would test him in ways he could never have imagined, pushing him to the very brink of his limits. And as he stood there in the darkness, a sense of foreboding washed over him, for he knew that the true test of his strength was yet to come.

4

A Glimpse of Power

As dawn broke over the horizon, Michael Stone emerged from the ancient mansion, the orb of power clutched tightly in his hand. The trials of the night had tested his resolve, pushing him to the brink of his limits and beyond. But as he stood bathed in the soft light of the rising sun, a sense of exhilaration coursed through his veins. He had passed the first test on his journey towards unlocking his inner potential, and nothing could stand in his way.

With a newfound sense of purpose, Michael made his way back to the city, the orb pulsing with an inner light in his hand. As he walked, he couldn't shake the feeling that he was being watched, that unseen eyes followed his every move. But he pushed aside his fears, focusing instead on the task at hand.

As he reached the heart of the city, Michael found himself drawn towards a bustling marketplace, its streets teeming with life and energy. Here, among the throngs of people, he would find the next step on his journey—a chance to harness the power within him and unleash it upon the world.

With a sense of anticipation building in his chest, Michael wove his way through the crowd until he came upon a small stall nestled in the corner of the square. The stall was adorned with all manner of trinkets and baubles, each one shimmering with an otherworldly light. But it was the figure standing behind the counter that caught Michael's attention—a wizened old woman with eyes that sparkled with an inner fire.

"Welcome, traveler," the old woman greeted him, her voice a melodic whisper that seemed to dance on the wind. "I sense that you carry great power within you, a power that yearns to be unleashed. But first, you must learn to harness it."

With a knowing smile, the old woman beckoned for Michael to approach, her eyes alight with a wisdom that seemed to transcend time itself. And as he drew closer, she reached out and placed a hand upon his chest, her touch sending a jolt of electricity coursing through his veins.

"Close your eyes, young one," she whispered, her voice barely more than a breath. "Feel the power that resides within you, waiting to be set free. Let go of your doubts and fears, and embrace the truth of who you are."

With a deep breath, Michael obeyed, closing his eyes and surrendering himself to the darkness. And as he did, he felt a surge of energy enveloping him, swirling around him like a cyclone of raw power. Images flashed before his mind's eye—visions of worlds beyond his wildest imaginings, of possibilities unbound by the constraints of reality.

But amidst the chaos, a single image burned bright—a vision of himself, standing tall and proud atop a mountain peak, the world at his feet. And in that moment, Michael knew with a certainty that bordered on divine revelation— he was destined for greatness, destined to lead from within and unleash his inner potential upon the world.

With a sense of awe and wonder, Michael opened his eyes, the world around him bathed in a radiant glow. The old woman smiled knowingly, her eyes twinkling with pride.

"You have taken the first step on a journey of infinite possibility, young one," she said, her voice filled with a sense of reverence. "But remember—true power lies not in the strength of your abilities, but in the courage to wield them wisely. Go forth, and may the light of your inner potential guide you on your path."

And with those words echoing in his ears, Michael turned and walked away, the orb of power burning bright in his hand. For he knew that the trials ahead would test him in ways he could never have imagined, but with the power of his inner potential as his guide, there was nothing that could stand in his way.

5

Betrayal

The city streets were bathed in the soft glow of twilight as Michael Stone made his way through the bustling crowds. His heart swelled with newfound confidence, the orb of power pulsing with energy in his hand. But beneath the surface, a seed of unease began to take root—a nagging sense of doubt that refused to be silenced.

As Michael navigated the winding alleyways, his thoughts drifted back to Marcus Blackwood, the enigmatic mentor who had guided him on his journey thus far. Something about their last encounter had felt off, a subtle shift in the air that left Michael feeling unsettled. But try as he might, he couldn't shake the feeling that Marcus was hiding something—something dark and dangerous that threatened to tear their fragile alliance apart.

Lost in thought, Michael rounded a corner and came face to face with a familiar figure—Sarah, a fellow traveler he had met on his journey towards unlocking his inner potential. Her eyes widened in surprise as she caught sight of him, a smile spreading across her lips.

"Michael," she exclaimed, her voice tinged with excitement. "I've been looking everywhere for you. I have something important to tell you."

Curiosity piqued, Michael followed Sarah as she led him through the labyrinthine streets, her pace quickening with each step. But as they neared their destination, a sense of foreboding settled over Michael like a heavy shroud. Something was wrong—terribly wrong—and he knew it with a certainty that sent shivers down his spine.

Finally, they arrived at a small, secluded alleyway, its walls looming like silent sentinels in the gathering darkness. Sarah turned to face Michael, her eyes wide with fear.

"I have to warn you, Michael," she said, her voice barely more than a whisper. "Marcus—he's not who you think he is. He's been lying to us, manipulating us for his own twisted purposes."

Shock and disbelief washed over Michael as Sarah's words sank in. Marcus, his trusted mentor, his guide on this journey towards greatness—could it be true? Could he have been deceived all along, blinded by his own ambition and desire for power?

Before he could voice his doubts, a sudden commotion erupted from the shadows—a group of figures emerging from the darkness, their faces obscured by masks and shadows. Panic surged through Michael's veins as he realized that he had walked into a trap—a trap set by Marcus himself.

With a sinking feeling in his chest, Michael turned to Sarah, but she was already gone, vanished into the night like a ghost. And as the figures closed in around him, he knew with a sickening certainty that he had been betrayed—betrayed by the very mentor he had trusted with his life.

But even as despair threatened to consume him, a flicker of defiance sparked within Michael's soul. He would not go down without a fight—not while there was still breath in his body and fire in his heart. With a roar of defiance, he raised the orb of power high above his head, its light casting long shadows across the alleyway.

And as the figures closed in for the kill, Michael unleashed the full force of his inner potential, a tidal wave of energy surging forth to meet them head-on. In that moment, he knew that the true test of his strength had only just begun, and that the road ahead would be fraught with danger and deception.

But with the power of his inner potential as his guide, Michael was ready to face whatever challenges lay in his path. For he knew that true greatness lay not in the absence of fear, but in the courage to stand tall in the face of adversity and fight for what he believed in. And as he braced himself for the battle ahead, he swore a solemn oath to himself—that no matter what trials awaited him, he would emerge victorious, his spirit unbroken and his resolve unwavering.

6

The Dark Night of the Soul

As the chaos of the alleyway faded into the distance, Michael Stone found himself adrift in a sea of uncertainty. Betrayed by his mentor and abandoned by his companion, he wandered the streets alone, his mind swirling with doubts and fears.

The city around him seemed to pulse with an ominous energy, its once-familiar streets now shrouded in shadows that whispered of danger and deceit. Every alleyway held the promise of a hidden threat, every shadow concealing a lurking danger.

With each step, Michael felt the weight of his betrayal pressing down upon him like a leaden cloak. How could he have been so foolish, so blind to the truth that lay hidden beneath Marcus Blackwood's charismatic facade? And what of Sarah, the companion he had trusted with his life? Had she been complicit in Marcus's deception, or had she too fallen victim to his lies?

Lost in his thoughts, Michael wandered aimlessly through the labyrinthine streets, the darkness closing in around him like a vice. But as the night wore on and exhaustion threatened to overtake him, he found himself drawn towards a familiar landmark—a dilapidated building on the outskirts of town, its windows boarded up and its doors locked tight.

With a sense of resignation, Michael approached the building and pushed open the creaking door, stepping into the darkness beyond. The air inside was thick with the scent of dust and decay, the only sound the echo of his footsteps on the worn wooden floor.

As he made his way through the abandoned halls, memories from his past flooded his mind—memories of a childhood spent wandering these very same corridors, searching for answers to questions he couldn't yet articulate. But now, as he stood on the threshold of his darkest hour, those questions loomed larger than ever before.

With a heavy heart, Michael climbed the staircase to the upper floors, the darkness closing in around him like a suffocating embrace. But as he reached the top, he was greeted by a sight that took his breath away—a single ray of moonlight filtering through a crack in the ceiling, illuminating a small alcove hidden in the shadows.

Drawn towards the light like a moth to a flame, Michael approached the alcove and found himself face to face with a mirror—a mirror that seemed to shimmer and shift with an otherworldly energy. And as he gazed into its depths, he saw reflected back at him a vision of himself—a vision stripped bare of pretense and artifice, a vision that laid bare the truth of who he was and who he was meant to be.

But alongside his reflection, Michael saw something else—a shadowy figure lurking in the darkness, its eyes burning with malice and contempt. It was Marcus Blackwood, his once-trusted mentor turned betrayer, a specter haunting the depths of Michael's soul.

With a cry of rage, Michael lashed out at the mirror, shattering its surface into a thousand glittering shards. But even as the fragments rained down around him, he knew that he could not escape the truth that lay hidden within him—that Marcus's betrayal had awakened something dark and dangerous within him, something that threatened to consume him from the inside out.

As he stood there amidst the wreckage of the mirror, Michael knew that he had reached a crossroads—a moment of reckoning that would define the course of his destiny. For he realized now that the true battle lay not in the streets of the city, but within the depths of his own soul. And as he braced himself to confront the darkness that lurked within, he knew that the road ahead would be long and treacherous, but that he would face it with courage and determination, for he was Michael Stone, and he would not be defeated.

7

The Test of Faith

The city lay shrouded in darkness as Michael Stone stood at the crossroads of his destiny, the shattered remnants of the mirror scattered at his feet. With each passing moment, the weight of his betrayal bore down upon him like a leaden weight, threatening to crush his spirit beneath its weight. But amidst the despair and uncertainty, a flicker of hope burned bright within him—a determination to rise above the darkness and reclaim his true destiny.

With a sense of purpose coursing through his veins, Michael set out into the night, the streets of the city stretching out before him like a labyrinth of shadows and secrets. But as he walked, a voice echoed in the recesses of his mind—a voice that whispered of doubt and fear, of the uncertainty that lay ahead.

"Are you prepared to face the truth, Michael?" the voice taunted, its words dripping with malice. "Are you prepared to confront the darkness that lurks within you, or will you cower in the shadows like a frightened child?"

With each step, the voice grew louder, its words echoing in Michael's ears like a sinister refrain. But he refused to be swayed by its insidious whispers, for he knew that true strength lay not in the absence of fear, but in the courage to face it head-on.

As he ventured deeper into the heart of the city, Michael came upon a towering edifice—an ancient cathedral that seemed to pierce the heavens themselves. Its spires reached towards the stars, their silhouettes etched against the backdrop of the night sky like the fingers of some long-forgotten deity.

With a sense of reverence, Michael stepped through the cathedral's towering doors and into the hallowed halls beyond. The air was thick with the scent of incense and candle wax, the flickering torches casting long shadows against the stone walls.

As he made his way towards the altar, a figure emerged from the darkness—a priest clad in robes of deepest black, his face obscured by the folds of his hood. With a solemn nod, the priest motioned for Michael to approach, his eyes burning with an inner fire that seemed to pierce straight through to Michael's soul.

"You seek answers, my son," the priest intoned, his voice low and resonant. "But the path you walk is fraught with peril, a test of your faith and resolve. Are you prepared to confront the darkness that lies within you, to face the demons that haunt your every step?"

With a sense of trepidation, Michael nodded, his heart heavy with the weight of his doubts and fears. But even as he spoke the words, a sense of determination burned bright within him—a determination to prove himself worthy of the challenges that lay ahead.

And so, with the priest as his guide, Michael embarked on a journey of self-discovery—a journey that would push him to the very brink of his limits and beyond. Through trials of fire and trials of faith, he confronted the shadows that lurked within his own soul, battling against the forces of darkness with every ounce of strength he possessed.

But as the night wore on and the darkness threatened to consume him, Michael found himself tested in ways he could never have imagined. For the true test of faith lay not in the absence of doubt, but in the courage to believe—to believe in oneself, to believe in one's purpose, and to believe in the power of redemption.

And as the first light of dawn broke over the horizon, casting its golden glow upon the city below, Michael emerged from the cathedral's hallowed halls a changed man. For he had faced the darkness that lurked within him, and in doing so, he had found the strength to rise above it—to embrace his true destiny as a leader, a warrior, and a champion of the light.

8

Into the Abyss

The night hung heavy over the city as Michael Stone stood at the precipice of his destiny, the weight of his past and the promise of his future converging in a tumultuous whirlwind of uncertainty. With each breath, he felt the pull of the abyss—the yawning chasm of his own subconscious, beckoning him to confront the shadows that lurked within.

As he gazed out into the darkness, a sense of trepidation gripped him, threatening to paralyze him with fear. But deep down, he knew that he could not turn back—that the only path to true enlightenment lay through the depths of his own soul.

With a steely resolve, Michael took a step forward, plunging into the darkness with a single-minded determination that bordered on madness. The world around him dissolved into a swirling maelstrom of color and sound, the boundaries of reality blurring until all that remained was the echo of his own heartbeat, pounding like a drum in the depths of his mind.

As he journeyed deeper into the abyss, Michael encountered visions of his past—memories long buried, traumas left unhealed. Each image was a dagger to his soul, reopening wounds that had never fully closed, forcing him to confront the pain and suffering that had shaped him into the man he had become.

But amidst the darkness, a single light burned bright—a beacon of hope amidst the shadows, guiding him towards a truth that had eluded him for so long. And as he reached out to grasp it, he felt a surge of power coursing through his veins, filling him with a sense of purpose and clarity that he had never known.

With newfound strength, Michael pressed on, delving deeper into the recesses of his own subconscious with a sense of urgency that bordered on desperation. But with each step forward, the darkness seemed to grow denser, the shadows closing in around him like a vice, threatening to swallow him whole.

Just when he thought he could go no further, Michael stumbled upon a chamber bathed in an ethereal light—a sanctuary amidst the chaos, a respite from the storm that raged within. And there, at the heart of the chamber, he found himself face to face with a figure shrouded in darkness—a specter from his past, a reflection of his deepest fears and insecurities.

With a trembling hand, Michael reached out to touch the figure, his fingers brushing against its icy form. And as he did, he felt a surge of recognition—a dawning realization that the darkness he sought to conquer was not some external force, but a part of himself that he had long denied.

With a cry of anguish, Michael faced the specter head-on, confronting the shadows that lurked within with a courage that bordered on madness. And as he did, he felt a weight lift from his shoulders, a burden that he had carried for far too long finally cast aside

As he emerged from the abyss, Michael felt reborn—a phoenix rising from the ashes of his own despair, a warrior forged in the fires of his own inner turmoil. And as he stepped back into the light of day, he knew that the journey was far from over—that the true test of his strength lay not in conquering the darkness, but in embracing it, and in doing so, finding the light that lay hidden within.

9

The Confrontation

The city was bathed in the soft glow of dawn as Michael Stone emerged from the depths of the labyrinth, his mind reeling from the trials he had faced within. The echoes of his journey reverberated in his soul, haunting him with their lingering presence. But amidst the chaos of his thoughts, a singular purpose burned bright—a determination to confront his betrayer and reclaim his destiny.

With each step, Michael felt the weight of his resolve pressing down upon him, driving him forward with an unstoppable force. But as he neared his destination, a sense of apprehension gnawed at his gut—a primal instinct warning him of the danger that lay ahead.

The streets of the city were deserted at this early hour, the silence broken only by the sound of Michael's footsteps echoing off the cobblestones. But as he rounded the final corner, he was greeted by a sight that sent a shiver down his spine—a figure standing in the shadows, waiting for him with a malevolent glint in his eyes.

It was Marcus Blackwood, his once-trusted mentor turned betrayer, his face twisted into a sneer of contempt. And as Michael locked eyes with him, he knew with a sickening certainty that the time for words had passed—that the only language Marcus understood was that of violence and betrayal.

With a roar of defiance, Michael charged forward, his fists clenched in righteous fury. But Marcus was ready for him, his movements fluid and precise as he danced away from Michael's blows with the grace of a seasoned predator.

The two adversaries circled each other like prizefighters in the ring, their movements a blur of speed and aggression. But with each exchange, Michael felt the darkness within him stirring, threatening to consume him with its insidious whispers.

With a cry of anguish, Michael unleashed the full force of his inner potential, a wave of energy surging forth to meet Marcus head-on. But Marcus was no ordinary opponent—he was a master of the dark arts, a sorcerer wielding powers beyond mortal comprehension.

As the two forces clashed, the air crackled with electricity, the ground shaking beneath their feet. But amidst the chaos, a single voice cut through the din— a voice that spoke of redemption, of forgiveness, of the power of love to overcome even the darkest of evils.

It was Sarah, Michael's companion and confidante, standing tall in the face of danger with a courage that defied comprehension. And as Michael locked eyes with her, he felt a sense of clarity wash over him—a realization that true strength lay not in the mastery of one's own power, but in the willingness to stand by those we hold dear, no matter the cost.

With newfound determination, Michael renewed his assault, channeling the energy of his inner potential into a single, devastating blow. And as his fist connected with Marcus's jaw, he felt a surge of satisfaction—the sweet taste of victory mingled with the bitter sting of betrayal.

But even as Marcus crumpled to the ground, defeated and broken, Michael knew that the battle was far from over—that the true test of his strength lay not in vanquishing his enemies, but in forging a new path forward, one built on trust, compassion, and the unwavering belief in the power of redemption.

As the sun rose over the city, casting its warm embrace upon the world below, Michael stood victorious, his spirit unbroken and his resolve unwavering. For he knew that no matter what trials lay ahead, he would face them with courage and conviction, secure in the knowledge that the light of his inner potential would guide him on his journey, illuminating the darkness and leading him towards a future filled with hope and possibility.

10

The Dawn of a New Beginning

The first rays of dawn crept over the horizon, painting the sky in hues of pink and gold as Michael Stone stood atop a hill overlooking the city. His journey had been long and arduous, fraught with danger and deception, but as he gazed out at the world spread out before him, he felt a sense of peace settle over him—a peace born of hard-won victory and the promise of a new beginning.

With each breath, Michael felt the weight of his past lifting from his shoulders, the shadows that had haunted him for so long dissipating like morning mist in the light of day. But amidst the sense of relief, a nagging doubt lingered—a question that had plagued him since the beginning of his journey: What lay beyond the horizon? What new challenges awaited him in the ever-unfolding tapestry of life?

As if in answer to his silent query, a figure emerged from the shadows—a familiar face, worn with the passage of time but still radiant with an inner light that seemed to defy explanation. It was Sarah, Michael's companion and confidante, her eyes shining with a quiet resolve as she approached him with a sense of purpose.

"Michael," she said, her voice soft but firm. "The journey we have undertaken together has been fraught with peril, but through it all, we have remained steadfast in our belief in the power of redemption and the strength of the human spirit. Now, as we stand on the brink of a new beginning, I cannot help but feel a sense of hope—a hope born of the knowledge that no matter what trials may come our way, we will face them together, as allies and friends."

Michael nodded, his heart swelling with gratitude for the companionship and support Sarah had offered him throughout their journey. Together, they had faced down the darkness that lurked within and emerged stronger for it, their bond forged in the crucible of adversity and tempered by the fires of their shared experiences.

With a sense of determination burning bright within him, Michael turned his gaze towards the horizon, his mind filled with visions of the future that lay ahead. And as he did, he felt a surge of excitement coursing through his veins—a sense of possibility and potential that filled him with a newfound sense of purpose.

For though their journey had been long and difficult, Michael knew that it was only the beginning—that the true test of their strength lay not in the battles they had fought, but in the challenges that lay ahead. But with Sarah by his side, he knew that they would face whatever trials came their way with courage and conviction, secure in the knowledge that the light of their inner potential would guide them on their path.

As the sun rose higher in the sky, casting its warm embrace upon the world below, Michael and Sarah stood together atop the hill, their spirits soaring on the wings of hope and possibility. For they knew that no matter what the future held, they would face it together, united in their belief in the power of redemption and the promise of a new beginning. And as they set out on their journey once more, they did so with hearts full of hope and souls ablaze with the light of their inner potential, ready to embrace whatever challenges lay ahead and forge a destiny worthy of their dreams.

11

Shadows of Doubt

The city bustled with life as Michael Stone and Sarah ventured forth into the unknown, their footsteps echoing off the cobblestone streets like a heartbeat in the night. Despite the sense of peace that had settled over them in the wake of their victory, a shadow of doubt lingered in the depths of Michael's mind—a nagging uncertainty that refused to be silenced.

As they wandered through the labyrinthine streets, Michael couldn't shake the feeling that they were being watched—that unseen eyes followed their every move, lurking in the shadows like predators stalking their prey. But try as he might, he couldn't pinpoint the source of his unease, the tendrils of doubt winding their way through his thoughts like ivy on a crumbling wall.

With each passing moment, the sense of unease grew stronger, a palpable tension hanging in the air like a storm on the horizon. And as they turned down a narrow alleyway, the feeling of being watched intensified, sending a shiver down Michael's spine.

Suddenly, without warning, a group of figures emerged from the darkness, their faces obscured by masks and cloaks. Instinctively, Michael reached for the hilt of his sword, his heart pounding in his chest like a drumbeat in the silence of the night.

But before he could react, the figures surrounded them, their movements fluid and precise like dancers in the shadows. And as they closed in, Michael caught a glimpse of their eyes—eyes filled with malice and contempt, eyes that seemed to pierce straight through to his soul.

With a sinking feeling in the pit of his stomach, Michael realized that they were outnumbered, outmatched, and outgunned. But even as fear threatened to overwhelm him, he refused to back down—not while Sarah stood by his side, her courage unwavering in the face of danger.

With a cry of defiance, Michael charged forward, his sword flashing in the dim light of the alleyway. But the figures were ready for him, their movements like a well-choreographed dance as they parried his blows with ease.

For what seemed like an eternity, the battle raged on—a whirlwind of steel and shadow, a symphony of clashing blades and grunts of exertion. But as the minutes turned to hours, Michael felt the tide of the battle turning against them, his strength waning with each passing moment.

Just when all seemed lost, a voice called out from the darkness—a voice filled with authority and command, a voice that sent a chill down Michael's spine.

"Enough," the voice boomed, cutting through the chaos like a thunderclap. And as the figures melted back into the shadows, Michael caught sight of their leader—a figure clad in armor, his face hidden behind a mask of cold indifference.

With a sense of resignation, Michael lowered his sword, his breath coming in ragged gasps as he struggled to regain his composure. But even as he sheathed his weapon, he knew that the true battle had only just begun—that the shadows that lurked within the city held secrets far darker than he could have ever imagined.

As they made their way back onto the main thoroughfare, Michael couldn't shake the feeling that they were being watched—that unseen eyes followed their every move, lurking in the darkness like ghosts from a forgotten past. And as they disappeared into the night, a sense of foreboding settled over him like a heavy shroud, a harbinger of the trials that lay ahead.

12

The Veil of Deception

The city lay cloaked in darkness as Michael Stone and Sarah navigated its labyrinthine streets, their senses alert for any sign of danger lurking in the shadows. The encounter with the mysterious figures in the alleyway had left them shaken, their nerves raw with the knowledge that they were being hunted by forces they did not fully understand.

As they made their way through the winding alleyways, Michael couldn't shake the feeling that they were being led into a trap—that every turn, every twist of fate, brought them closer to the jaws of a predator waiting to strike. But try as he might, he couldn't shake the feeling of unease that gnawed at his gut like a hungry beast.

With each passing moment, the tension in the air grew thicker, a palpable sense of foreboding settling over them like a heavy shroud. And as they rounded a corner, they came face to face with a figure cloaked in shadow—a figure whose presence sent a chill down Michael's spine.

It was Marcus Blackwood, his once-trusted mentor turned betrayer, his eyes burning with a malevolent light that sent a shiver down Michael's spine. And as he locked eyes with Marcus, he knew with a sickening certainty that they had walked straight into the lion's den—that the true test of their strength lay not in physical combat, but in the battle of wits that lay ahead.

With a sense of resignation, Michael and Sarah approached Marcus, their movements slow and deliberate as they prepared to face their fate head-on. But even as they braced themselves for the confrontation that lay ahead, a voice whispered in the recesses of Michael's mind—a voice that spoke of doubt and uncertainty, of the possibility that all was not as it seemed.

As Marcus began to speak, his words laced with honeyed promises and half-truths, Michael felt a surge of anger rising within him—a righteous fury born of betrayal and deception. But amidst the chaos of his emotions, a single question burned bright in his mind: Could he trust his own instincts, or were they merely a product of the paranoia that had taken root in his soul?

With a sense of determination burning bright within him, Michael listened as Marcus spun his web of lies, each word dripping with venom and deceit. But even as the doubt threatened to consume him, he clung to the flicker of hope that still burned within his heart—a hope born of the belief that truth would always triumph over deception in the end.

With a sudden burst of clarity, Michael saw through Marcus's facade, his eyes narrowing with determination as he prepared to unveil the truth hidden beneath the veil of deception. And as he confronted Marcus with his lies, he felt a sense of liberation wash over him—a weight lifted from his shoulders, a burden cast aside in the face of the undeniable truth.

But even as Marcus's lies crumbled around him, Michael knew that the battle was far from over—that the shadows that lurked within the city held secrets far darker than he could have ever imagined. And as he and Sarah made their way back into the night, a sense of foreboding settled over them like a heavy shroud, a reminder of the trials that lay ahead. But amidst the uncertainty, a single truth remained—no matter what dangers awaited them in the darkness, they would face them together, united in their belief in the power of truth, trust, and the unwavering light of their inner potential.

Milton Keynes UK
Ingram Content Group UK Ltd.
UKHW050435280324
440101UK00016B/1107

9 788686 872043